To school library media specialists—

because a library is the heart of a school

Vanessa Weiss, Classmate

It's amazing how much dying can do for a girl's popularity.

I mean, I'm sitting here in the funeral parlor watching Erin McCall and my other classmates standing around Raquel Falcone's dad, each one of them acting like Raquel's best friend. I don't know if Erin's just doing her usual center-of-attention thing, or if she's actually trying to make Mr. Falcone feel better. That's what you do for a dead person's family—tell them she'll be missed even if you never once had a nice word for her or about her.

I know what I'm talking about: I was there in homeroom when Mrs. Bellanca broke the news.

She told us all to sit down, and I have to believe that was at least partly so she could see where the empty desk was—I don't think she was exactly sure which one to connect Raquel's name to. Certain kids have a tendency to be invisible.

"I'm afraid I have some bad news for you," Mrs. Bellanca said.

Her plan to prepare us did the opposite. I couldn't have been the only one who suspected that another standardized test was about to be announced. Or an assembly, because the administration had decided that the first springlike day of the year was a good time to talk to us about the evils of drugs, alcohol, bullying, or sex. Or maybe, since it *was* a nice day, there was going to be a fire drill; a certain number are required each semester, but the principals in upstate New York generally try to schedule them for days without snow and ice rather than run the risk of personal-injury lawsuits.

A little chatter of speculation started as people tried to guess what the bad news could be.

Mrs. Bellanca rapped her knuckles against the

desk to get our attention—one step up from middle school, where they have this little rhythmic hand-clap thing they do to get the students to quiet down.

"I'm sorry to have to tell you," Mrs. Bellanca said, "that the school has suffered a loss." Which still could have been something minor. She might have meant that one of the teachers was going on maternity leave—or one of the students. (Though usually there's no official word on *those* situations.) But then she finally came out and said it: "Raquel Falcone was killed in a car accident last night."

People glanced around. Even after seven months of classes together, they had to look to see who was missing, who Mrs. Bellanca meant.

I knew immediately. Not that Raquel was a particular friend of mine or anything. I sit behind her in homeroom, so I'd already noticed she wasn't there, because I could see Mrs. Bellanca without having to crane around Raquel's bulk.

My first thought, on hearing that Raquel was dead, was: *Oh, crap. That makes me the class fat girl.*

Which lets you know—just in case there was any doubt—exactly how nice I am.

So now, all those kids who couldn't have been bothered to talk to Raquel when she was alive are leaving flowers at the little impromptu shrine at the street corner where the car hit her. They're taking up a collection to buy a Raquel Falcone memorial park bench to put on the school's front lawn. And they've even started a letter-writing campaign to get the speed limit lowered on that stretch of Poscover Road to prevent further accidents—even though nobody's 100 percent sure what happened. Why should not knowing what happened stop anybody from commenting . . . or crusading?

They say she was leaving a movie, talking and laughing. Maybe Raquel stepped off the curb without watching what she was doing.

Maybe someone jostled her—which leads to two more questions: Was it accidental? Or intentional?

Or maybe Raquel knew exactly what she was doing when she stepped in front of that car. Maybe she'd had enough of being nobody's particular friend, of being "that fat girl" in ninth grade.

A fast, fatal step to popularity is a possibility to keep in mind.

But meanwhile, I'm happy to note that Lindsay Lapjani might actually look wider than I do. She says she's not fat—it's a cultural thing. And I'm certainly not going to be insensitive enough to bad-mouth anyone's culture.

Angela Bellanca, Teacher

All those years of schooling. All those years of paying off the loans for that schooling. Years that stretched out because teachers are notoriously underpaid.

As opposed, for example, to my sister Emily, who went into business communications—whatever, exactly, that means.

Never mind, I know what it means. It means she has beautiful clothes because she doesn't have to be on her feet all day in a building where, in the winter, the heat doesn't quite make it to the third floor; and, in the summer, there is no air-conditioning because the voters turned down the building-improvement bond, figuring there aren't many days that we'd need it. Try standing in front of thirty bored ninth graders on a June afternoon and then tell me you don't need air-conditioning. And, yes, my shoes look orthopedic. That's because they *are* orthopedic. The girls make snide remarks about them based on what styles they're wearing. The boys are always trying to look down my neckline or up my skirt. And they're *all* eyeballing the size of my butt if I'm wearing pants. As far as hair, Emily gets hers done every week to maintain what she calls "that nice professional look." For a teacher, "professional" means not a ponytail. Except on those days when we really need that air-conditioning—then a ponytail is fine.

Not that I'm complaining: I didn't fall into being a teacher; I chose it as my career. I wanted to make a difference, and usually I don't compare myself to Emily. Except when she sits us down in front of the computer at some family function and makes us check out the latest digital photo album of the latest wonderful vacation she and her husband have taken. Meanwhile, my husband and I have had to postpone for another year getting a new car, since the old one doesn't really stall and leave me stranded all *that* often.

"I will make my classes interesting," I told myself when I was studying. "I will have a multitude of lesson plans, to reflect the strengths and interests of each year's incoming students."

I anticipated endless energy. I anticipated making learning fun. I anticipated students who could, eventually, be won over.

I never pictured students who refused to give me half a chance, or parents who wouldn't come to parent-teacher conferences, or buying supplies with my own money because the district is—yet again—on an austerity budget.

And I never pictured myself having to tell a classroom full of kids that one of them had died.

Joey Nguyen, Custodian

Articles removed from locker #3245, Falcone, Raquel M.:

algebra book (level 1)

world studies book

biology book

3-ring binder (marked DEADLY BORING NOTES ON DEADLY BORING CLASSES)

1 artist's sketchbook (marked TOP SECRET, KEEP OUT LEST THE CURSE OF THE DEADLY LAKE ONTARIO SEA-KELPIES BE UPON YOU)

1 white mitten (left hand)

1 pink glove (right hand)

pamphlet from NutriSystem

receipt from 24 Hour Fitness

mechanical hamster that plays "Yankee Doodle"

do-not-resuscitate order, from Highland
 Hospital, not filled out

Hayley Evenski, Best Friend

Raquel and I met in first grade when our teacher, Mrs. Scarborough, arranged us alphabetically. I was fortunate to have Raquel sitting behind me because at that point in my life my parents didn't realize I needed glasses. When Mrs. Scarborough would write on the board, I'd tell her that I couldn't read her handwriting, and she took that as a personal criticism of her, rather than as evidence of a problem with my eyesight.

She told me to concentrate and to try harder.

Raquel, however, began leaning forward and—very quietly—reading out loud whatever Mrs. Scarborough had written on the board.

Lucky for me, Raquel was both kindhearted and a good reader.

In second grade, our teacher, Mr. Thesing, suggested to my parents that they might want to take me to have my eyes checked, which was when I got glasses. But I figured I was forever in Raquel's debt. Mrs. Scarborough, I was sure, would have kept on insisting that I wasn't trying hard enough, so there's a good chance I'd still be in first grade if it hadn't been for Raquel.

Not that her kindhearted deeds always worked out. In third grade the two of us dabbled at being Brownies, and Raquel talked the troop into going to Harborview Manor Nursing Home to sing Christmas carols to the residents. The attendants wheeled all these old people into the front room. I mention the wheelchairs so that you understand our audience hadn't necessarily volunteered to come. Mrs. DeLuca was the troop leader, and she also was the one who played the piano. She played, we sang, and most of the old people snoozed right through our performance. Except for one little old lady who covered her ears and moaned repeatedly, "Make them stop."

To this day Raquel will insist we were a major hit.

Oh damn.

Jonah Proia, Potential Date

I was thinking of inviting Raquel to next week's spring formal.

Of course, first I asked Stacy Galbo, even though I knew it was a real long shot, her being the most popular girl at Quail Run High.

"Oh, that's sweet," she said in a voice that made my knees wobble. "Thank you, but I already have a date."

I looked down at the lunch tray I was carrying, so she wouldn't see the disappointment on my face. "Okay, sure, I understand," I said. "I shouldn't have waited so long." It wasn't that I'd waited *that* long; the dance was still a month away at that point. But

I know girls like to plan these things years in advance. In any case, I'm not sure how much of what I said she heard, because by the time I looked up, she'd walked away.

"Did you ask her?" Ned demanded before I even set my tray down at our table. I should have never admitted to anybody that I'd planned to talk to her at lunch that day. Yeah, well, *admitted* isn't exactly the right word. Ned and Paul had been pressuring me all week to either put up or shut up about inviting Stacy. I know them well enough to suspect there was money riding on whether I'd ever actually get up the nerve to invite her.

Now Paul, reading my face, said, "*Ahh,* she turned him down."

Ned glanced from me to Paul and back to me, as though Stacy turning me down was inconceivable.

"Yup," I admitted, concentrating more than was absolutely necessary on opening my milk carton.

"How come?" Ned asked.

"Waited too long," I said. "She's going with somebody else."

"Who?" Paul asked.

I shrugged.

Paul snorted, obviously suspecting that Stacy Galbo would lie to get out of going with me, as though she'd risk not going at all rather than go with me.

The next girl I asked was Zoe Kanisky. While Stacy is the most popular girl in the ninth grade, Zoe is the best looking. She's got this incredible blond hair, and blue eyes, and boobs she's not afraid to show off. I cornered her in the library's reference section while Mrs. Shesman was busy checking out books before the bell rang at the end of the period.

"I'm sorry," Zoe said, her eyes big and innocent. "Who are you?"

Maybe it was the new haircut I'd gotten the day before. "Jonah," I reminded her. "Jonah Proia."

"I'm sorry," Zoe said, even more brightly than before. "Who are you?"

At least I knew enough not to wonder if this was a case of sudden-onset hearing-and-seeing loss. Erin McCall and a couple of the other girls were listening in, always a bad sign, and snickering, an even worse sign.

Zoe asked, "Are you, like, on the football team?"

I couldn't think of anybody on the football team who she could possibly mistake me for.

"No," I admitted.

She laughed, still sounding friendly. Too friendly. "Well, and we can certainly see that you're not on the basketball team."

Translation: Jonah Proia is short and dumpy.

"Could you, perhaps, be a member of the yearbook staff? Or on the forensics team? Or in the drama club? Is your daddy rich? Is there any reason I should even be talking to you?"

No, no, no, no, and—sigh—no.

I slunk away before Zoe's friends could gather any more people to personally witness my ego being ground into dust. It was bad enough knowing that everybody would soon enough be *hearing* about it.

Lest anyone call me quick, the third girl I asked was Joyce Lin. Even though we were in the hallway, between classes, she stopped and pulled out a notebook and pen.

"P," she spelled out loud, "R, O, I, A. Right?"

"Yeah . . ." Surely it didn't bode well that she had to write down the name of her date. On the other hand, she hadn't needed to verify my name, just the spelling.

She was counting—the days till the dance? I wondered. But when I leaned in to look at her notebook, there wasn't a calendar, but a list.

"Seven," she told me.

"Seven what?"

"You're boy number seven to invite me to the dance—chronologically. But if I rated by preference, you're much higher, so there is a chance. If something should happen to . . ."—she studied the page—"four of these other boys, I'll be happy to go with you." She snapped the notebook shut and left me to figure out for myself if I should be depressed for getting scorned, or relieved that there were two boys lower on her list than me.

Which was better shape than Erin McCall would

leave me in. Even though Erin had seen my humiliation at Zoe Kanisky's hands, she was the fourth girl I invited to the dance because she's almost as beautiful as Zoe, but not quite as mean. Or so I thought. Erin called me an ugly toad. "Like I would want a formal picture taken with you," she said.

Which I extrapolated to mean "No, thank you."

That night I must have been kind of mopey, because my mother kept after me.

"I'm fine," I told her all through dinner.

Later, when I was doing my chem homework on the couch in front of the TV, she came and sat next to me. "What about that dance?" she asked. Geez, a dance is just the kind of thing a mother gloms on to—while setting the recorder for a show that airs while I'm away just slips right through her mental grasp. "You going?" she asked.

"Nah," I said.

"Don't tell me you haven't asked that girl yet—what's her name? Suzy?"

"Nobody's named Suzy anymore," I told her.

But she couldn't be deflected that easily. My

mother's the kind of person who likes to solve problems. *Facilitate* is the word she uses. If I said I'd changed my mind about asking Stacy, Mom might well have called Stacy herself to try to facilitate a date with her.

"Stacy's real popular," I said. "She's going with someone else. *All* the popular girls are already going with someone else." Because I was feeling sorry for myself, I added, "I'm not good-looking enough for the popular girls to bother with."

"You are very good-looking," my mother insisted.

"For a toad," I muttered.

My mother kissed the top of my head. She said, "You are a handsome boy who will grow up to be a handsome man."

She's my mother. It's her job to think that.

"Well . . . ," my mother started, in what I recognized as her about-to-facilitate tone.

"What?"

"Why don't you call that girl who helped you with math last June?"

"Raquel?" I asked.

Raquel had tutored me for the final two weeks of school, after our teacher had pointed out that I needed to get an 87 on my final exam. Otherwise I'd flunk math and have to take it over in summer—and I wouldn't be allowed to graduate with the rest of my eighth-grade class.

"She was nice," Mom said. "I remember how the two of you would get to laughing. But at the same time, she helped you grasp those math concepts."

"Yeah, but, Mom—*Raquel*?"

"I'm just saying," Mom said, standing up to head back to her reading chair, "someone who can make you laugh might be a better choice for a date than someone who calls you a toad."

Ned and Paul would mock me something terrible. They'd point out that Raquel was about as big as all the other girls I'd asked, rolled into one.

Which she wasn't. Not exactly.

And that's how my *friends* would react.

Still, I thought of how Raquel had come over every evening for two whole weeks. Made math fun. And understandable. The morning of the exam, she gave me a little white feather and told me that as long as I held on to it, I would ace the test; and that—in a pinch—I could also use the feather to make me fly.

I'd actually walked into the test grinning. The only bad thing was Paul had asked me why. When I'd tried to explain, he'd gone "Huh?" So I'd had to spell it out: "You know, like Timothy Mouse giving Dumbo the feather for his self-confidence." And Paul had said, "Yeah? You've got the big ears for it, but which one of you really looks most like Dumbo?"

But, feather or tutoring, I'd gotten an 89 and passed the test and graduated with all my friends.

I still have that feather—somewhere.

I thought of Erin rejecting me because I wouldn't look good enough in the photographs.

"Maybe," I told Mom.

That was last week. And I was, seriously, thinking of inviting Raquel to the spring formal.

Raquel's Blog

Welcome, traveler, to Gylindrielle's World.

Things I like:

- Sword of Mawrth (Of course—Sword of Mawrth is part of my world as Gylindrielle. But Gylindrielle's World is kinder, gentler, greener, and happier than the Sword of Mawrth world. No running amuck with swords or barbed weapons, or even barbed tongues allowed. No denizens of Hades welcome. In Gylindrielle's World, all friends are true, and all food is nonfattening. Dragonflies are intelligent and friendly, birds don't poop, corners are not sharp, Christmas is never disappointing, and root beer is free.)

Hmm, I'm having trouble thinking of anything else I like. I'll have to come back to this. Meanwhile, let's move on to:

 Things I hate:

- mean people
- homework
- homework assigned by mean teachers
- hospitals
- hospital workers who are mean
- snack food that tries to pretend it's not that bad for you by labeling for impossibly small servings—like: 3 potato chips. Yeah right.
- weather that's too cold (meaning below 68 degrees)
- weather that's too hot (meaning above 72 degrees)

- hairdressers that don't listen to what you want—for example, Julie at the Hair Emporium: WHAT WERE YOU THINKING?
- mosquitoes that whine in your ear at night. I mean, if you're going to suck my blood, go ahead and do it. When I'm in bed, I'm too tired to try to find you anyway. But must you gloat and keep me awake?
- oh yeah—and did I mention MEAN PEOPLE?

So, welcome to my world. Feel free to look at my drawings. (Each one is labeled as to medium, and if there's a story behind it.) Feel free to comment, but only if you have nice things to say. Am I telling you that I'm the kind of person who only wants to hear good things about herself? Well, *duh*! I'm guessing you are, too—but maybe you're just too shy to admit it.

A special welcome to everyone from the Sword of Mawrth boards. I am ALWAYS ready to talk about the game.

Meanwhile, if you've got no life of your own and you've got time to kill, go ahead and read my ramblings.

POSTED 3 DAYS AGO:

TUESDAY/08:03PMEDT

Our school is having a big dance next week. I don't know why I got it into my head that it might be fun to go. I mean, it's not like I can dance, or like I want to spend even MORE time with my classmates than I am legally mandated to by New York State, or like I'm into the music the rest of the people my age listen to and talk about, or like I want to hear ANY music at a volume that has been scientifically verified to liquefy a human brain so that you can't carry on an intelligent conversation but are reduced to that horror-of-all-horrors: SMALL TALK.

- "Lively music, huh?"
- "Good snacks, huh?"
- "I like what you did with your hair. No, I said *hair.* HAIR. *HAIR.* Never mind."

So why did I want to subject myself to that? Maybe I have a brain tumor that has skewed my ability to reason. But something got me thinking that it might be fun, and something got me thinking that maybe someone would ask me to go, and then something got me thinking that it's only a week off. Maybe—can it be possible?—maybe NO ONE will invite me after all, and if I'm to go, I'll have to go unescorted. Solo. By myself. Wallflower. Dead meat. Women and small children, avert your eyes from the sight. But at least then I won't have to worry about the dreaded SMALL TALK. Because in all likelihood NO ONE will talk to me anyway. I can keep those deep thoughts about the music and the food and anybody's hair to myself.

I have come to a conclusion—and at the same time I have a newly formulated GOAL in LIFE. Next time Mrs. Bellanca assigns one of those essays she's so enamored of, I can submit this:

WHAT I SEE FOR MY FUTURE

by Raquel Falcone

I will never have a boyfriend, so I will no longer obsess. Instead, I will take in stray cats for companionship. I will become the prototypical CAT LADY every neighborhood has (or should have). I will specialize in ugly or deformed cats, but—since they have had a hard enough life as it is—I will not have them neutered or spayed. (The little critters need to have *some* fun.) This, of course, will result in more cats, which is fine because my short-term goal is to make myself a nuisance to my neighbors with offending smells, noise, and clutter. Eventually I will die, but since I have no friends to care about me, no one will notice, and my cats will feed upon my body. Which brings me to my long-term goal: contributing to what the Walt Disney Studios

Philosophy Department has so eloquently termed The Circle of Life.

THE END

Feel free to comment.

current mood: cranky, with dramatic overtones of self-pity

Responses to this thread:

TUESDAY/08:27PMEDT

COMET GIRL: Comment? *Comment?* Several fallacies there, Raquel, including that—if you will recall—I taught you how to dance when we were in 4th grade. Don't blame me if you can't remember how.

Fallacy # 2 is that you have no friends to care about you. Excuse me? What is this friendship bracelet with your name on it that I have dangling from my wrist? Just because you've forgotten that I taught you to dance is no reason to deduce that I am no longer your friend.

Fallacy # 3 is that your choices for this dance are:

- get invited
- go alone
- don't go

We are living in the 21st century. *You* can invite someone, you know.

Fallacy # 4 is that cats will turn on a master who has died and eat her. I have read on this matter. It's all a matter of timing. *Dogs* will eat a dead master—usually several days after the demise, when they have reached the point of starvation, usually after tearing up the house, looking for any other food and/or a way out. *Cats,* on the other hand, do not wait for a master to die, but will try to eat anyone who has stopped moving. This is why you should never let a cat sleep with you on your bed. Unless you're a restless sleeper, the cat is likely to mistake you for dinner.

TUESDAY/08:43PMEDT

GYLINDRIELLE: Heya, Hayley.
I suppose it is a pretty crappy goal all around. Animal control would come in and destroy all the cats, cause nobody would want to adopt them for fear that they'd developed a taste for human flesh.

P.S. No way am I going to invite a boy to a dance, regardless of the century.

P.P.S. Your teaching me the chicken dance and the hokey pokey—while very thoughtful—does not qualify me to dance in public.

TUESDAY/08:50PMEDT

COMET GIRL: Excuse me. The chicken dance and the hokey pokey are the building blocks upon which all other dances are built. Check out MTV to verify.
As far as those cats with a taste for human flesh,

maybe that girl from your school who's so big into causes could step in and rescue them after you kick the bucket—what's her name?

TUESDAY/08:51PMEDT

GYLINDRIELLE: Mara Ravenell

TUESDAY/08:53PMEDT

COMET GIRL: Yeah, her. (Mara Ravenell—sounds like a Sword of Mawrth name!) She could develop a whole Save the Human-Flesh-Eating Cats Program.

TUESDAY/07:55PMCDT

WARRIORGUY: Hey, Gylindrielle. If I lived three or four states closer to New York, *I'd* take you to that dance. You're just the kind of girl I've been looking for!

TUESDAY/08:59PMEDT

GYLINDRIELLE: That's very sweet, Warriorguy.

But don't forget that after the first time you propositioned me, I read the background information you have posted on the Sword of Mawrth boards, and I know that—besides living in Warrensburg, Missouri—you're twelve years old. I'm sure that you're very cute for a twelve-year-old stalker, but this just isn't going to work out.

TUESDAY/08:04PMCDT

WARRIORGUY: C'mon, Gylindrielle! Being stalked by a 12-year-old stalker is better than being stalked by a 53-year-old stalker!

TUESDAY/09:09PMEDT

GYLINDRIELLE: Be still my heart! Warriorguy, you need to bear in mind that I do not look like my Sword of Mawrth avatar.

TUESDAY/09:11PMEDT

COMET GIRL: NOBODY looks like their Sword of Mawrth avatars. Manga art exaggerates everything. Even *Barbie's* boobs-to-waist ratio would improve in manga.

TUESDAY/08:13PMCDT

WARRIORGUY: You could post a picture of yourself as Raquel.

TUESDAY/09:14PMEDT

GYLINDRIELLE: Good night, Warriorguy. :)

 *current mood:* greatly improved—thanks

TUESDAY/09:16PMEDT

GYLINDRIELLE: BTW, the second-run theater around the corner is playing that animated film festival—lost track and 9:30 is the last show. Join me, Hayley?

TUESDAY/09:18PMEDT

COMET GIRL: Can't, cause *I* would need someone to drive me. And my parents are definitely not in a Good Mood. But enjoy!

TUESDAY/08:19PMCDT

WARRIORGUY: Have a great time. And think of me.

TUESDAY/09:20PMEDT

GYLINDRIELLE: GOOD NIGHT, Warriorguy.

Hayley Evenski, Best Friend (Part 2)

I keep thinking: What would have happened if I'd gone with her?

The thing is, I don't love those animation festivals the way Raquel does.

Did.

There are usually a couple of funny or moving features, a few Very Strange ones from Europe that I have no idea what they mean, and a whole bunch of really lame stuff that I'm pretty sure I get—but I'm left thinking: So what?

Then again, was my avoiding ninety minutes of animation worth Raquel's life?

Because in the end, I probably could have worn

my parents down; I probably could have gotten one of them to drive me to the theater. They always liked Raquel, and they knew it was hard on us, being assigned first to different middle schools, then going to different high schools. So they *might* have driven me.

And if they wouldn't have—but I had tried—then I wouldn't feel so much that it was my fault.

Not that, if they'd said no, it would be their fault.

But . . .

I don't know. It's just too confusing.

I want to blame someone.

But I seem to be the only one around to blame.

Could I have stopped whatever it was that happened from happening?

Shouldn't a best friend be able to do that?

The police say she stepped off the curb into the path of an oncoming car.

At 11:10 on a Tuesday night on Poscover Road there isn't *that* much traffic, so there was some speculation—you could tell by the way the first reports were worded—that she *may* have done it intentionally: suicide by second-party driver.

That really made me mad, because there's *no way* Raquel would have done that. She had too much respect for herself, and besides, she would never inflict that onto some poor driver, someone she didn't even know. It must have nearly killed Mr. Falcone to hear those insinuations. Finally, though, the police told him there was no reason to declare her death a suicide.

My brother, Tyler, who loves a good conspiracy, pointed out that knowing Raquel the way we do—we know she wouldn't commit suicide. But since there wasn't much traffic, we had to assume either that Raquel had been darn unlucky to step off the curb *just* as a car was coming—or that someone had pushed her.

Tyler was a good deal of the reason my parents were in a bad mood that night, so if I were inclined, I might say it was partially his fault I didn't go with Raquel to the movies.

Except that's really, really stupid.

Tyler's theory is really, really stupid, too. There were four witnesses there that night—a retired couple and a pair of college boys. None of them knew Raquel, and she wasn't the kind of girl you could take such an instant dislike to that a stranger would just push her into oncoming traffic. All four of them said the same thing, according to the police who interviewed them: They were laughing and talking about one of the animation shorts, and the next thing anybody knew, Raquel was off the curb. . . .

I don't want to think about that part of it.

Actually, I don't want to think about any part of it, but my mind keeps going back to that moment over and over, like some kind of instant replay loop in my head.

She could have fallen. Raquel was *not* the most graceful person around.

She could have been distracted and not seen the car. Raquel could be a little spacey.

If I had been there, I might have prevented whatever happened.

If I had been there, at least I might *know* what happened.

Albert Falcone, Father

Did I tell her that night to stay safe?

It was kind of a joke we had. Every morning as we did our getting-ready-for-the-day dance around each other in the kitchen—me on my way to work, her ready to run for the school bus—I would always say, "Have fun today. And stay safe."

Sometimes, Raquel would come back with something like "Oh drat! Why did you have to say that? Today was the day I was planning on being reckless, and now I can't. And here I was toying with the idea of letting myself get kidnapped by crazed aliens with rectal probes."

But now I'm wondering: Did I tell her that night to stay safe?

I know my words have—had—no magic power to protect her, but still, the thought that I might not have wished her well haunts me.

That I let her go out at night doesn't bother me, though I've heard the snide comments suggesting I am not a good father because my fourteen-year-old daughter was out at eleven o'clock at night. Raquel is—was—a couple weeks short of being fifteen. She was very responsible, and the theater is so close—down two well-lit blocks, around one corner, and across one street.

Across one street.

Across one damn street.

Six minutes to walk there. I know because we've walked there together countless times. Raquel loves—loved—movies. Especially animation.

It was almost 9:30 when she came running downstairs shouting, "The animation festival! It starts in eight minutes, and if I don't go now, there will *never* be another chance to see it!"

"It's a school night," I reminded her.

"I've done all my homework," she told me.

Raquel always did her homework. Sometimes on the bus or between classes the day it was due, but she always got it done. She was a good student.

"It'll be on DVD in another couple months," I said. I'd already taken my shower. I was in my pajamas and had settled down with a book and didn't want to get dressed again.

"DVD's not the same as the big-screen experience," she wheedled. "You don't have to come with me. It's only ninety minutes. I'll be home and in bed asleep by eleven-thirty." She must have seen that I was considering, because she added, sounding like her uncle Theo, the lawyer, "Whereas if you don't let me go, then I'll be grumpy and thinking about what I missed, and tossing and turning all night in my bed, and I'll end up getting *less* sleep than if you just let me go. Not to mention the strain on our father/daughter relationship." She glanced at her watch and was bouncing up and down. "They hardly show any trailers on weeknights. I'm going to miss the beginning. Please-please-please-please-*please*?"

I *must* have told her to stay safe, because she was worried about being late. I would have pointed out that they *always* show coming attractions, and that she had plenty of time to get to the theater carefully.

Her last words to me: "You're the best, Dad"—as she leaned over me in the armchair to kiss me good-bye on the forehead.

My last words to her: "Yeah, yeah"—spoken in a disgruntled tone.

My last words should have been: "Stay safe, baby girl."

Carmella Lombardini, Driver

It wasn't my fault.

Everyone says so. They've said it all along. The nice police officer said it that night.

None of it helps.

There are so many "what-ifs" that could have changed everything. What if Sharon's bridal shower had been at our house instead of at the maid of honor's mother's house? What if my car had a bigger trunk, so that I didn't decide it would be easier to use my husband's SUV to bring all the presents back to our place? What if I had more confidence driving that big boat? What if I had insisted on helping Kaylee's mother clean up afterward? What if

Sharon had come home with me rather than spending the night at Kaylee's? What if I had paid better attention while Sharon had driven us there, so that I would have learned the way as I went *to* the shower, while it was still sort of light out, and then I wouldn't have been constantly glancing at the handwritten directions as I drove home in the dark?

I'm pretty sure I wasn't looking at the directions when I passed that little plaza. Two blocks up there was a signal light, and I remember hoping it would turn red and stop me, which would give me time to check out those directions and verify if—at the next light—I was supposed to turn right or left.

There was a loud *thump.* The car lurched, sort of like I'd hit a pothole or bumped the curb. But I've done that before, and this was different.

Right away I knew I'd hit something. I hadn't seen anything, so I assumed a dog had run out into the street. I thought, *Oh no,* imagining someone's distress at losing their pet. I was already pulling over to the curb, looking into my rearview mirror, afraid of what I would find.

In the mirror, I could see a bunch of people on the right-hand corner I'd just passed. Someone on the curb screamed.

One last moment of blissful ignorance: I thought, *It isn't bad enough that I run over someone's dog—I have to run over someone's dog while he and his friends are watching?*

And then I saw it wasn't a dog.

It wasn't my fault.

I never saw the people on the curb. Even so, you can't always be driving like the people on the curb are going to leap out at you.

I never saw the girl.

I *know* I never saw her.

So why—every time I close my eyes—do I see her face looking at me through the windshield?

Mara Ravenell, Head of the Keep Our Streets Safe Campaign

I'm the acknowledged expert at Quail Run High when it comes to petitions, solicitations for a movement, sponsored walks for a cause, or any other kind of social activism.

Mostly I've participated in events of a national nature—MS Challenge Walk, handing out ribbons for Mothers Against Drunk Driving, collecting baby clothes for Birthright. I even organized a knit-off for Project Linus. I got a yarn store to donate yarn, and talked an office supply place into free photocopying so that I could provide baby blanket patterns in three knitting proficiency categories: beginner, intermediate, and expert. We ended up with thirty-seven blankets to donate to charity. Pretty good for someone who doesn't even knit!

I'm also an expert at letter-writing campaigns. I know when it's appropriate to write to your senators, or to your congressmen, or to the governor.

But now I'm working on a definitely local project: trying to get the speed limit down to thirty on Poscover Road or—at the very least—to have a stop sign put in at the corner of Poscover and Williams. People go tearing down Poscover Road like it's a major highway, without taking into account that sections of it are residential, and without taking into account that little kids live in some of those houses. It was obviously a danger to Raquel Falcone, but it's a danger to a lot of other people, too.

So I've got some petitions—each worded slightly differently—that I've had my volunteers drop off in the vestibules of area churches and hang on the bulletin boards at supermarkets, the athletic club, and nearby restaurants. I figure we'll leave them for one week—then get those babies back before they become clutter and get tossed out.

At the same time, I also had my volunteers write five letters each. (They were supposed to make all five sound different, and they weren't supposed to confer with one another. So hopefully the letters will sound like they're coming from a wide variety of sources. I mean, it's good for *me* to be organized, but we don't want the movement to look like a movement—more like a spontaneous outpouring.) Each volunteer was then sent door-to-door in the Poscover/Williams area—where people would most likely be willing to sign a letter.

I thought it would be a good idea to have Raquel's parents sign letters, too, but it turns out she only has a father, and he was a bit too foggy to sign. "I'll just take it," he said. "I'll read it later and send it in myself."

Okay. Whatever. That means he'll lose out on the opportunity to have us take care of faxing it in for him—because another step in my make-it-simple-for-the-petitioners plan is to hold a raffle to raise money for faxing. A local toy store donated a stuffed unicorn for the raffle prize (which is perfect because somebody told me Raquel loved all that fantasy-type stuff).

I trust it's going well, though I haven't paid as much attention to the follow-through of this campaign as I usually do. I've been reading about the wonderful work done by the Heifer Project, where families in poor countries are given a pair of animals to raise so that they can use the products from the animals (fur from the llamas, eggs from the chickens, etc.). Then, as the animals reproduce, the family can sell them or use them for meat. It's a wonderful program to get people to be self-sufficient, while treating them with trust and dignity. I think it would be just great if we could mobilize the student population here at Quail Run to donate enough money to buy a pair of oxen for some family in Africa. Don't you?

Esther Struk, Neighbor

I remember the first time I saw the Falcones.

Old Mrs. Steinmiller next door had fallen down once too often, and her kids moved her to a nursing home. You can just shoot me—thank you very much—before you send me to one of those places. Two daughters and a son, and not a one of them could find room in their fancy-schmancy houses out in the suburbs for the woman who had brought them into the world and done without to give them the best, even after her husband had died while they were still in school?

But anyway, old Mrs. Steinmiller was finally gone. The next thing I know, there's one of those

U-Hauls parked out in front of the house, and about fifteen different people toting furniture and boxes in. They had so many helpers, they got in one another's way more than they helped.

Oh lordy, I remember thinking, *I wonder how many of this crew is actually moving in?*

It's not that I don't like Greeks or Italians—both represented by that family—but these Mediterranean types tend to have big, noisy families. Sometimes there'll be several generations in one house, with the grandmother from the old country not speaking a word of English but always chattering at you in a disapproving tone, and more kids than you can shake a stick at. So I was wondering.

Eventually, I learned that there were only the three of them moving in: Al (representing the Italians) and Cleo (part of the Greek contingent), and their daughter, Raquel, who was about five at the time. While the rest of them went in and out of the house, they put her in the fenced-in backyard. I thought she was too young to be left unattended. *One of those so-called helpers should stay with her,*

I thought. If they were counting on me to keep an eye on her, I was too busy.

But every time I glanced out the window, she was doing fine all by herself—she didn't try to get out of the yard, and she didn't climb on the fence, and she didn't yank the leaves off my crab apple tree where it hangs close to the fence, the way Mrs. Steinmiller's grandchildren always did.

Raquel seemed perfectly capable of amusing herself. She had a little tambourine, and she was dancing and spinning around—not loud and look-at-me, just totally self-sufficient. Which isn't something you can say about many kids these days.

Now that, I told myself, *is a girl who will never be bored or lonely.*

Erin McCall, Head of the Committee for the Raquel Falcone Memorial Bench

I met Raquel the summer between elementary school and middle school. There's this annual festival on the grounds of Maplewood Middle. A lot of the teachers, parents, and students run the various games and activities, and it's considered this big community-building thing. But besides the duck pond and the clown dunk (which is actually a principal dunk, an idea I think more schools should embrace) and the various games of chance to win baked goods and stuffed animals and assorted junk you probably wouldn't buy at the dollar store, besides all that, somebody knows somebody, so there are also a few actual carnival rides.

My mom had been part of the bake sale committee since I was seven because she believes in networking and wanted to make sure everyone knew and respected the McCall family long before my brother or I would be attending Maplewood. It was a way for her to keep her finger on the pulse of the school that was "the heart of the neighborhood"—those would be her words, not mine. My words would be: She wanted to know which were the teachers whose kids got the highest scores on the standardized tests. That way she could pull strings to make sure we ended up in those classes, so that we would be well prepared for the best area high school, so that we would be well prepared for the best colleges, so that we would get high-paying jobs that would be prestigious enough for her to tell people about and wouldn't leave us still living at home when we were thirty like our cousin Walter.

But here it was, after all those years of prep time, the summer festival of what was now my middle school.

Mom was making sure the apple crumb cakes

and berry pies and other assorted goodies the volunteers had made were all coming in and being properly stored or displayed to their best advantage. She had bought all-day tickets so Seth and I could go on the rides as often as we wanted. Not that we were hanging out together. He's three years younger than I am and was roving the festival grounds with his pack of friends. Any time our paths crossed, I tried my best to pretend we weren't related.

I was with my best friends Stacy and Zoe. We had gone to Neil Armstrong Elementary together, and we would be going to Maplewood Middle together in another three weeks.

But for now, Zoe was having a problem with her bra and wanted us to all go to the ladies' room while she pulled herself back together. We had just been to the ladies' room—where there had apparently been a problem of another nature shortly before.

"It's stinky in there," I complained. "Can't you adjust your bra out here?"

"Shh," Zoe hissed, waving her arm and attracting

more attention than my lowered voice had. When we were eleven, the word *bra* caused us all to go a bit frantic.

I offered, "Nobody'll see if you face this wall and we stand around you."

Zoe rolled her eyes and said, "*Everyone* will guess *exactly* what's going on."

"I'll go with you," Stacy volunteered.

I knew I was supposed to say I would, too, but I couldn't bring myself to. "I'll save a place in line for us at the Roundup," I said.

So they went off in one direction, and I went to the Roundup, where, miraculously, they were just loading up for the next ride and there was no line.

Well, it makes no sense for me to wait at the head of a nonexistent line, I told myself, so I climbed on.

I must have sampled a few too many of the baked goods because as soon as we started to spin, I got woozy. *Don't throw up,* I told myself, because on the Roundup the centrifugal force keeps you from moving, even from lifting your hand. If I threw up, I could imagine that chunk of barf hanging suspended in front of my face until the ride ended, at which point it would probably go *fwap!* right back onto me.

Of course I needed to get *that* image out of my head because it was making me even more inclined to lose my lunch—what you would call a self-fulfilling prophecy.

But somehow or other I managed to keep my eyes closed, my teeth clenched, and the contents of my stomach in my stomach.

Why is it that when you're enjoying the ride it's over almost as soon as it's started? But if you're hating it, the ride operator seems to get in a generous mood and gives you at least a dozen extra rounds?

Eventually the Roundup slowed, then finally stopped.

I still couldn't move. Even with my eyes squeezed shut, I could feel the world revolving around my head.

The ride operator called out to me that if I wanted another ride, I had to get off and go through the line again.

As if.

"You all right?" someone asked. An adult's voice—a woman's.

"I'm going to die," I was able to mumble.

It was a mistake. I should never have opened my mouth. My stomach contents made a break for it.

I leaned over and heaved, spewing hot dog and brownies and cookies and Sno-Kone and funnel cake all over several nearby sneakers. Two pairs of feet hastily backed up. The adult pair stayed by me. In fact, the voice that went with it assured me, "It's okay, don't worry, everything is fine," and I felt a comforting arm around my shoulders.

I also heard the ride operator go "Oh man!" but the woman hugged me and said again, "It's okay, it's fine."

"I just threw up," I wailed.

The woman said, "And I bet you're feeling better for it."

I considered.

She was right.

The world had stopped spinning, my head no longer felt about to explode, and my stomach was calming down even as we spoke.

I was finally able to focus on her. Her hair was red, though obviously—by her coloring—not naturally. My mother would have pointed out that she was too plump for her own good. At the moment, though, her squishiness was comforting, like being hugged by a teddy bear. There were two girls with her—one wearing glasses, the other looking like a miniature, darker-haired version of the woman. Three weeks later I would meet Raquel again in middle school, but at the time I didn't know her. Friend or relative, the other girl, the one with the glasses, must have gone to a different middle school, because I never saw her again.

Anyway, Raquel's mother gently led me off the Roundup and had me sit on the grass. She pulled a container of wipes out of her purse and handed me a couple to clean off my chin. She also gave me a piece of gum to rid my mouth of the taste of being sick. Miraculously, I hadn't gotten any vomit on my clothes, though Raquel needed a wipe for her leg where I'd gotten a bit on her, and her friend was rubbing the side of her sneaker on the grass to clean it off. Neither girl was making a fuss about what I'd just done—what I'd just done on them.

"I'm so sorry," I told them.

Raquel said, "Everyone's puked some time or other."

Glasses-girl said, "Of course, some more spectacularly than others."

Raquel's mom asked me, "Is your mother around?"

"Yes," I admitted. But I didn't want them walking me inside the gym. I didn't want the baked-foods committee looking at me like I was a war casualty that needed explaining. So I didn't tell her where my mom was. "I'm fine now." I stood and saw Stacy and Zoe come walking around the Roundup together, looking for the end of the entrance line. "And there are my friends."

"Are you going to be going to Maplewood in September?" Raquel's mom asked me.

I nodded, and her mother said, "Raquel, too."

"Great," I said. "See you," and I walked away, intercepting Stacy and Zoe before they could be brought into the conversation. I took one by each arm and headed them toward the games of chance. Zoe and Stacy both had their noses wrinkled.

"Eww, what's that smell?" Zoe asked.

"Someone threw up on the Roundup," I said, chomping energetically on my gum to release the wintergreen scent. The ride operator had tossed a bucket of water on the nasty heap I'd made, which spread it out more than cleaned it up, but he took down the entrance chain to let people on again.

"Eww," Zoe repeated. "I'm not going on that."

"Exactly," I agreed.

Stacy asked, "Was it that chubby girl?"

I could have said no. I could have said it was some other girl who had been on the ride near us, some other girl I could no longer see in the crowd. But I didn't think of that. I just thought how embarrassed I'd be if they knew it had been me.

So I said, "Yes."

Zoe said, "Fat girl's probably been eating all afternoon. No wonder she barfed." Even though Raquel wasn't really fat then, just a bit round.

"That's Raquel Falcone," Stacy said. "She lives down the street from me."

Even hearing that Stacy knew Raquel didn't make me fess up—I'd be revealed as a liar, which was even worse than being revealed as someone with a weak stomach who'd upchucked on innocent bystanders after a carnival ride.

"Eww," Zoe said yet again. "I hope that doesn't mean she'll be coming to school here."

Oh, yeah. Even though I'd responded to Raquel's mother, I hadn't really thought of that.

But it was definitely too late to admit anything.

I owe you, Raquel, I thought. *I owe you big.*

But I never paid her back.

Vanessa Weiss, Classmate (Part 2)

I'm still sitting here in the funeral parlor, and I'm regretting my choice of clothing.

I figured I had to wear black to be respectful, but I'm not a black clothes kind of girl. I have a pair of Levi's that started life black, but they're gray now—and not even dark gray. So I borrowed my mother's black skirt, even though it was too tight. I managed to get it buttoned, but really it was cutting me in half at the waist. Still, I figured I could put up with a bit of discomfort in honor of my dead classmate. Besides, it wasn't like I was going to be eating or dancing or anything but sitting in it.

Though breathing, occasionally, might be nice.

My choice of black tops was also limited. There's one sleeveless souvenir T-shirt I have that says OCHO RIOS, JAMAICA/NO PROBLEM, MON. Not appropriate, I decided. One of my other tops is gauzy and has sparkles, which seemed a bit overdone for a funeral service. The last is black velvet, and when I tried it on at home it went perfectly with the skirt. I figured it might be a bit warm for May, but by evening the temperature would dip and I'd be fine.

I looked good at home, and in the car while my mother drove me here, and as she dropped me off by the front door. Then I walked into the funeral parlor.

Right beyond the front door at the Bauleke and Morrow Funeral Home, they've got this big ornate mirror that takes up half the wall. Why? I have no idea. As if people who are in mourning want to see themselves puffy-eyed and red-nosed. I caught my reflection, and saw that the black of my velvet top was a totally different black from the black of my mother's skirt.

They looked hideous together.

Okay, I told myself, *the lights have to be bright out here because people are coming in from outside, and the management doesn't want anyone tripping over the doorway or the edge of the rug or anything.*

Maybe, I thought, *in the actual room where the body is laid out, they will have the lights dim so as not to be too bright and cheery.*

Turns out the light in this room could probably give a person a tan.

I'd never seen an actual dead person before, and I wasn't eager to see one now. Thinking maybe I could work myself up to it—or not—I avoided the end of the room where the casket was set, surrounded by more flowers than I'd ever before seen indoors. I was amazed at the number of people, too, but it was too late to leave. My mom wouldn't be back for another forty minutes. There were a lot of sofas and chairs, so I headed for one and sat down in the hope that no one would notice my mismatched outfit.

Suddenly, I felt the waistband button of my mother's skirt give. I hoped it had just unbuttoned.

Yeah. What were the chances of that?

The thing was so tight, I was fairly certain it wouldn't fall off me, even with the top button gone, but since there were ten buttons going down the front, I was also fairly certain my mother would throw a hissy fit if I came home one button short because that would mean she had to either search out a store that carried a matching one, or change all of them.

I looked on the floor. But of course, no button. Deciding it must have rolled under my chair, I stood—taking care to adjust my velvet top over the waistband so no one would see I'd popped a button—and I got down on my knees to feel around on the rug.

Nothing.

People were trying not to look at me. They probably thought I was praying for Raquel but was too dumb to find the casket.

I got up, accidentally stepping on the hem of the skirt, and the button—which had been caught in the folds of fabric all along—fell to the floor and rolled under the chair.

Once again I genuflected and reached under the chair. Retrieved the button. Stood. Caught, once again, the trailing edge of the skirt. Felt it shift slightly southward, and threw myself into the chair before it could end up around my ankles. Knocked my elbow against the dried flower arrangement on the table by the chair. Caught vase and flowers before anything actually hit the floor, and only broke a couple of the stems by grabbing too tight. Stuffed them back in the vase, and set the vase back on the table. Hoisted the skirt back up to my waist.

I wasn't moving again, I thought, till it was time to leave. And until then, I would fervently pray that most of the other people would go first, before my mother arrived.

This was when I noticed how warm it was.

Much too warm to be wearing a velvet top.

Which was what my mother had suggested at home, but my lack of clothing options had made me hope she'd be wrong.

Don't think about it, I told myself. *Think about something else.*

So now I'm sitting here hating my clothes, realizing that there isn't much to think about—nothing that you *want* to think about, anyway—when you're at a funeral home for a girl you hardly knew and everybody you *do* know is clustered around the front of the room, talking to the dead girl's father or looking in fascinated horror into the open casket and saying such things as "She looks good, doesn't she?"

Hello?

I mean, I haven't checked, but doesn't she look *dead*?

I run my finger around my black velvet neckline, trying to get a little air circulating.

It doesn't help, but I try it a few more times.

I happen to look down and notice that tiny fibers have shed off the velvet top and are now adhering to my sweaty hands. The effect is like a multitude of stunted eyelashes. I can only assume they are also adhering to the exposed area of my neck and upper chest, where they probably give the impression of being stubble. Wonderful. People will assume that I am not only overweight but incredibly hairy and in the habit—though haphazardly—of shaving my entire torso.

I wipe my hand on the skirt and then run my hand over my neck and chest. I'm sweaty and sticky, and I'm wondering if I could have by chance touched my face and left a black fuzzy trail there as well.

The more I think about it, the more my face itches.

I make sure my hands are defuzzed before checking. No velvet fibers come off my face, but that could be because my sweat is making them cling.

I start to go through my purse. I know there's a mirror in there somewhere, but it seems to be buried under packets of Lactaid (because I'm lactose intolerant) and tampons (because—regardless of what they told you in health class about twenty-nine-day cycles—a girl knows that her period can start at any time).

There *is* that huge mirror in the front hall, but I don't want to get up—hairy and sweaty and with my skirt apt to fall off—so I continue pawing through my purse. Empty gum wrappers and a clump of hair from my hairbrush escape my lap and land on the floor at my feet.

Finally, I find the mirror. It's facedown and covered with lint, but by now I'm accustomed to using my mother's skirt to clean things.

My face is flushed and sweaty, but there is no velvet residue. I wipe some of the sweat off. Otherwise, anyone who sees me looking in the mirror will think I am conceited and can't get enough of myself. Then I run a finger under each eye so that no one can mistake my sweat for tears. I don't want to look like a hypocrite like Zoe and Meg and Aretha, who are carrying on about how much they'll miss Raquel.

I *do* notice, however, just as I'm about to drop the mirror back into my purse, that my neckline is red and irritated.

Is that from being overheated and the velvet chafing? I wonder. But only for a second.

I catch myself rubbing my palms on the skirt—not to clear them of velvet—but because they are itchy.

I check my palms. Sure enough, they have little red itchy bumps on them. Familiar little red itchy bumps. Because it isn't bad enough that I'm overweight and lactose intolerant—I'm also blessed with allergies. I'm guessing that something in that dried flower arrangement has set me off. And I've just touched near my eyes, which will make them start to itch and water.

I lean back in the chair, thinking *Why me?* and my head makes an audible *bump* against the wall.

I glance around to see if anyone has noticed.

Mara and her crowd still have Mr. Falcone cornered, so that's good. Mrs. Bellanca is chatting with a couple of the boys who have just walked in.

There's only one person looking my way, a girl I don't know. She's kind of red-eyed behind her glasses, and for a moment I hope she hasn't noticed me. She's raised her hand to her mouth, and I wonder if she's one of Raquel's relatives, and if she's about to start really crying.

Sigh.

Then I see—what she's doing is trying not to laugh.

Paul Phillips, Classmate

I don't understand girls.

Last week nobody liked Raquel Falcone much.

As far as the guys were concerned, if she'd been one of those fat girls who are desperate, she wasn't so fat that a guy would have turned her down. If there'd been a few pounds less of her, you would have said she was kind of cute. She was smart without being in-your-face smart. I mean, it wasn't like she had her homework at every single class or waved her hand when she knew the answer. And she was funny when she spoke up—which wasn't often—the kind of funny that didn't make you worry that tomorrow it would be directed against you. So, all in all, Raquel was the kind of girl who—if she was your sister, you wouldn't have been embarrassed.

So, as far as the guys were concerned, you could take her or leave her.

Except . . .

Big *except* here . . .

EXCEPT: The other girls didn't like her.

Not understanding girls and all, I couldn't say why. It wasn't like she was competition for any of them or anything. I mean, she wasn't the smartest, or the funniest, and—with or without the weight—she wasn't *that* cute. And besides not having the looks, she didn't have the clothes, or the voice, or the moves, or most especially: The Attitude.

Girls can be merciless.

Tough? Girls have got guys beat on that any day.

Nobody had to say anything—you just knew: If you were the kind of guy who missed those cues, who would talk to Raquel, you might just as well have a big LOSER tattooed onto your forehead.

But now, all of a sudden, it's Poor Raquel, and

Sweet Raquel, and No-I-Never-Talked-to-Her-in-School-but-She-Was-My-Role-Model-and-Best-Bud Raquel. They're gloomy in the halls and writing solemn poems for her for the school paper and buying teddy bears to leave by the road where she died. I think Mara Ravenell is talking to someone in the Catholic Church to see about getting her nominated for sainthood.

I don't understand girls.

I didn't especially like Raquel, but I know well enough not to admit that now.

Zoe Kanisky, Classmate

I never knew anybody who died before.

Well, my grandfather—my father's father—died when I was about one, but that doesn't count. Someone who's only a year old doesn't really know anybody. In my grandmother's apartment, there are pictures of my grandfather, including one of him holding me in a blanket when I was a newborn. But I don't remember being a newborn, and I don't remember him: nothing, nada, zip, a total blank.

Sometimes I'll be watching an old movie, and I'll say to my mother, "That guy's kind of cute. Would he be like about a hundred now?" And she'll tell me, no, he died in a motorcycle accident, or of AIDS, or of some other thing she can't remember, but anyway he's dead. And I'll think, *How sad.* Or sometimes she'll say he's still around and making movies and she'll tell me some recent movie he's been in, and I've seen it, and I'll remember the part he played, and I'll go: Whoa, he IS like a hundred. Not to mention fat. And that's sad, too. Hard to say which is sadder: the beautiful young person who dies, or the one who doesn't.

Not that Raquel was beautiful. But she was young. She is—was—in fact younger than me. Mrs. Bellanca writes on the board who is having a birthday during the current month. My name was up there all November, sharing the month with Abigail Adams and Jamie Lee Curtis. Raquel's was this month, on May 31. It was still up there for two days after Raquel died: "May 31—Raquel Falcone—15."

Kind of unsettling in a spooky sort of way.

Finally, somebody said something, and Mrs.

Bellanca erased it. But you can still see the smudge mark where it was.

Kind of like Raquel.

Raquel's life as a smudge mark on the earth.

Did she see the car coming? Did her life flash in front of her like it does in cartoons? How badly did it hurt, and for how long? The newspaper said she was pronounced dead at the hospital. Does that mean she didn't die right away? And if she didn't, was she conscious? Did she know she was dying?

It gives me the creeps to think that one instant she was laughing and talking and probably thinking about what she was going to eat for her next meal, or maybe thinking about that birthday coming up in another two weeks, and then—*pow!*—all of a sudden she's a smudge.

It's gotten me to thinking: In the movies, you always know something like that is going to happen. You can tell by the dramatic music, or you can tell because the character has just said how happy and complete she is.

And then I started thinking about all those people who are killed in terrorist attacks. No eerie music foreshadowed that they were in some creepy terrorist's version of a movie.

I made the mistake of mentioning all this to my grandmother. Instead of saying something to make me feel better, she said I was right! She said that it was kind of funny how some people are concerned with the end of the world, when for any one of us the end of the world could be seconds from now.

Gee, thanks, Gramma.

So, all of a sudden I'm thinking: How will I know? What if my life is about to end—*bam!*—NOW?

Or now?

Or now?

Stacy Galbo, Classmate

Being the most popular girl in school isn't as easy as you might think.

A school takes its whole personality from the attitude set by the "in crowd," and that's quite a responsibility. Sometimes girls let the power go to their heads. They take as an example the catty, toxic girls in movies, because *there* it's funny—even though, in the movies, the popular girls are almost always the villains, and they get their comeuppance by either being one of the first victims of the crazed serial killer stalking the halls, or by being publicly brought down and humiliated by, of course, kids from the "out crowd."

Newsflash: There is no such thing as the "out crowd." That is a Hollywood construct.

You can be *in* (which is a select few), or you can be *not in* (which is the vast majority), or you can be *out* (but then you're not part of any crowd, because that's what "out" means).

But those popular girls who take Hollywood too much to heart and specialize in snide meanness—they can taint the entire school. (Are you listening, Zoe Kanisky?) The whole student body becomes disgruntled. The discontent spreads to the teachers and the administration, and then bounces back down on the students, intensifying the misery for all.

So I do my best to set a good standard, to be civil to all, and to talk behind the backs of only the outest of the out.

I didn't talk about Raquel, because there really wasn't anything to say. I thought that she was pathetic because she so obviously didn't even *try*—I mean how hard is it to lose *a few* pounds? And she wore her hair exactly the same every single day.

Never tried anything new to see what would have been more flattering.

The worst part—for me—was that she was always doodling. I was sure she was making fun of me, because a lot of times she was drawing what appeared to be a caricature of me: this thin-waisted, perky-boobed girl with big green eyes, and half of her body weight had to be that mound of blond hair that seemed to have a personality of its own. Since I have admittedly good blond hair, green eyes, and a figure I'm not ashamed of—I thought these drawings were supposed to be me. Maybe I'm a bit oversensitive, but the thing that settled it in my mind was that this girl in the drawings was always carrying—or waving—a big knife. Before she married my dad, my mother's name was Metzger, which is German for "butcher," and that's exactly what her father was—a butcher in a meat market. Which is not a sexy occupation at all. I thought Raquel had found out about that and was pointing out that my mother comes from a decidedly working-class family.

It was only when I saw Raquel's sketchbook at the funeral parlor, with pictures of this character—labeled *Gylindrielle,* which was apparently Raquel's alter ego—rescuing kittens and in other heroic poses, and with other characters drawn in the same style, that I finally realized she was not poking fun at me. She was, in fact, revealing a desire to look like me.

Now I feel terrible.

And I wonder: What would have happened if I had gone out of my way to be nice to her? If I hadn't just refrained from bashing her, but had tried talking to her—about hair and clothes and diet and stuff? Not enough contact with her to jeopardize my own standing, which I've worked so hard to attain, but enough to help her improve herself so she wouldn't be so sad and hopeless.

Would she not have stepped off that curb?

Because I have to think: Being her while wanting to be me—surely she stepped into the path of that car on purpose.

Police Report Addenda/Witness Statements

Thomas Yeager, student at MCC: It was so sad. One minute we were all standing on the curb, waiting for the chance to cross the street. Me and Diego, we had parked in the lot of that bicycle repair shop, Crawford's. It was after hours, so we figured we'd be okay even though the signs are all, like, VIOLATORS WILL BE TOWED, as if it makes any difference whether anyone parks there when the place isn't even open. The parking lot for the theater holds, like, about three cars, but in this case that woulda been okay 'cause nobody came, 'cause the movie was kind of lame, which was why it was in the second-run theater, anyway, but it was better than the movie that was playing at the student center. So that's what I was thinking about: How come the student center always plays such crappy movies that we gotta go to a second-run theater for entertainment? And wouldn't it make more sense to forget the movie entirely and just go get some pizza? But Diego, he's all into that cartoon stuff, and he's talking to this high school girl about how great it was, and there was this old couple there, too, waiting to cross the street, but I don't know where their car was 'cause it wasn't at Crawford's, and the girl—Raquel, they said her name was—she's talking to Diego a mile a minute about this one scene in the movie, waving her arms, and making moves like she's Xena, Warrior Princess, and the next thing I know, she's flailing her arms and falling off the curb, right in front of that car. That driver never had a chance to miss her.

Diego Mannillo, student at MCC: No, I don't think she fell. I think she never saw that car and she just stepped off the curb. Thomas was being kind of pissy because he didn't want to be there at all. He thought we shoulda gone for pizza or burgers. Food, not film. But the old guy, the girl, and me—we were talking about this one feature, this parody of *The Lord of the Rings* that was the best part of the festival. And we're repeating the funny lines to each other, and the girl, she's holding one arm out like she's brandishing a sword, and she's holding the other arm limp-wristed and she goes in this fruity kind of voice like the Legolas character had, "Stepping off into battle, now," which is what he kept saying, and that's when she stepped off the curb. So I gotta think she did it on purpose. But she never saw that car.

Edward Selby, 583 Clarkson Road: My wife and I didn't know any of the others. We just ended up together at the curb waiting to cross the street. Our car was behind the theater, but we were going to have some hot chocolate at that Greek restaurant next to the bike place before going home. My wife, she hadn't liked the movie and wasn't feeling well, which is why she didn't see what happened, and she was on my right-hand side. The one boy was standing off to the left, then the other boy—the one who was a pretty good mimic—then the girl, then me, then my wife, except that we were all kind of clustered—you know?—it's not like we were all standing in a row. The boy who was so good with doing different voices, he and the girl and I were having a good time pretending to be the various characters in the movie while we walked out of the theater and waited to cross. Then I think it's just like he said to the people from the restaurant: I think the girl just got overexcited and wasn't watching what she was doing. Such a pity. Such a terrible, terrible pity. It was awful to see. Terrible for the driver, too—she kept crying and saying, "It's not my fault." And it wasn't. The girl just stepped right in front of her. It was someone from the restaurant who called 911. They came running out when it happened. Awful. It's going to haunt all of us for a long time. It'll be so hard for the girl's parents. Must be terrible to lose a child. Just seems to be backward: Parents expect their kids to bury them. My wife's real shook up.

Marilyn Selby, 583 Clarkson Road: I didn't really see anything. I'm sorry. I wasn't paying attention.

Marilyn Selby, Witness

I'm afraid I killed that girl.

Does Edward suspect?

I heard him describe to the police how we were standing, and he said I was to his right. But I wasn't. I was to his left. I was between him and the girl. It isn't like Edward to misremember. I think he suspects, and he's lying to protect me.

The movie was too loud, and—at ninety minutes—it was at least forty-five minutes too long. I don't know if that *gave* me the headache, or if it just made my headache worse. As we were walking through the lobby, Edward suggested we go to the coffee shop across the street for a cup of hot chocolate so I could sit down and take some aspirin.

I don't know what was the matter with me that night. Edward was talking and laughing with the young people, and normally that's something I love about him, his youthful exuberance. But that night I was thinking he was prancing around like Errol Flynn in one of those old pirate movies, and I was thinking this was making my head hurt even worse. I went rummaging through my purse to look for the aspirin, so I could have it handy to pop into my mouth as soon as we got to the restaurant.

While I had my head down, the girl, also prancing, bumped into my purse. I was annoyed at all their foolishness—the endless movie, my headache, Edward acting like a teenager, me acting like a grumpy old woman—and I bumped back. Not hard. Not a great shove. Certainly with no intention of harm.

I'm trying to reconstruct in my head what happened. I never looked up, and it seemed as though several seconds passed while I continued to look for that aspirin bottle. And if that's true, then I didn't cause her to lose her balance and fall. If that's true, she bounced off me, continued to play, and then—nothing to do with me—she either fell or stepped off the curb on her own, as the two boys have said.

But I keep going back over it. Maybe only a heartbeat passed before that awful *thud.*

Maybe it wasn't *and then . . .* Maybe it was *and so . . .*

I watch Edward to see if he acts differently toward me.

There's nothing I can put my finger on.

I want to ask him: "Did you really think you were the one standing next to the girl who died?"

But if in the confusion he *did* remember incorrectly, my asking will make him wonder why I'm asking. It will make him wonder why—if I remember things differently from him—I didn't say so to the police.

And if he lied, then it's because he saw what I did, and he knows I killed her.

And I'm not sure I can deal with knowing that.

Marco Falcone, Cousin

I always thought Raquel was so lucky. I mean, she's an only child, and I have four sisters. Four. I'd trade all or any one of them for Raquel.

People are always looking at my four sisters—Amorette, who's nineteen; Gina, who's sixteen; Corinne and Sophia, the twins, who are fourteen; and me, eleven—and then they ask my parents, "So you kept on trying till you had a boy?"

Mom and Dad always smile, like whoever's asking is the first person in the world to ever come up with that, and they say, "No, that's just the way it worked out."

My sisters smile, too—while people are watching. In private, they pinch me—especially Corinne and Sophia. They have a way of working in tandem, one distracting me while the other zeros in with those fingers of iron. Gina generally prefers smacking me upside the head. Amorette goes, like, "So, what are we—chopped liver?" As if I'm the one responsible for tactless questions.

When girls grow up in a swarm, they grow up mean.

But I don't think Raquel would have been. She hardly ever got tired of playing Go Fish with me and never looked at my cards if I forgot to hold them up straight. Amorette has always claimed her cheating is a life lesson for me, like she's doing it for my own good rather than just to win.

Sure, Raquel was sort of fat, but we're Italian. Italians are *not* carb watchers. Meals have lots of pasta and bread, and everybody's mother makes about ten different kinds of cookies for any special occasion. Once they reach a certain age, Italian women take it as a personal insult if you don't eat. In our family, most of the aunts and uncles and the majority of the cousins older than twenty-five are what you could call hefty. My sisters, alarmed by the family photo albums, think they can fight their genealogy, and they're always on diets. Maybe that's why they're so mean.

Mom and Dad weren't sure if we kids should go to the funeral parlor.

"They went last year when Uncle Sal died," Mom pointed out.

"That was different," Dad said, by which I took him to mean Uncle Sal was practically in the *Guinness Book of World Records,* he was so old. They flew his ashes back from the retirement community in St. Petersburg, Florida, so that he could be buried next to Aunt Imogene, who had died so long ago even Amorette hadn't been born yet. So it wasn't like it was a surprise Uncle Sal had died. And it wasn't like we knew him.

When Raquel's mom, Aunt Cleo—who we of

course knew—died, we'd been on a weeklong cruise over winter break. We didn't even hear about it till we got back two days after she'd been buried.

So for Raquel, in the end Mom and Dad left it up to us whether we wanted to go to the funeral parlor. I would have voted no, but the frightful four wanted to go, so that made me feel like I had to.

The room was big, and full of aunts wearing *a lot* of perfume and uncles fighting back with equal amounts of aftershave, and about as many flowers as they put around the altar on Easter morning. My head began to swim as soon as we crossed the threshold.

There was a book, which Mom said she'd sign for all of us, and I asked a perfectly reasonable question: "What's the book for?"

Mom said, "So your Uncle Al will know we came."

"Isn't he going to be here?" I asked.

Mom gave me one of those that-was-a-weird-question looks, and Gina smacked the back of my head.

"Don't do that," Mom told her. She told me, "Of course he'll be here."

"Then why does he need the book?"

I dodged a second smack, so that Gina's hand accidentally made contact with the stand on which the book rested.

She clutched her fingers and swore, loudly, and the person who had signed the book right before us, an older woman I didn't know, turned around to glare.

"If you can't behave . . . ," Mom said in a low but threatening voice.

"It's *his* fault," Gina said. "Tell him it's not cute to keep asking dumb questions."

"Enough," Dad told her.

"I'm not—" I started.

"Enough," Dad told me, too.

The signing-in was only a stop along the way. The line continued, following the contours of the room, then passing by Uncle Al like a wedding receiving line, except that it ended just beyond him at Raquel's coffin. For the moment, I wasn't worrying about that last part. I was doing quite well at *not* thinking about Raquel. What I was worrying about was what I could possibly say to Uncle Al.

Relatives who'd been through already came to chat with us and keep us company. The adults called me "young man," with the uncles shaking my hand (as if attending a funeral made me into a grown-up, too) and the aunts giving me powdery pecks on the cheek. People asked Amorette how she liked college, and she answered, "Very much," which was a surprise considering all the complaining she does at home. They asked Gina if she was beginning to look at colleges yet, and she said she wanted to go to Vassar, but that Mom and Dad wouldn't even take her to look because of the expense. "State schools are fine," Dad would explain, to cut off any sympathy she might have gotten. And as far as Corinne and Sophia, people kept getting the two of them confused and then finding an infinite source of quiet amusement in that.

Mom leaned in close to Dad, but I could hear her when she whispered, "The casket is open."

That made me jump, because I thought she meant it was opening right then and there. But the lid was all the way up and nobody else seemed to be reacting.

Sophia, who's probably going to be a teacher when she grows up—either that or a spy, because she has such sharp eyesight that nothing gets by her—had of course noticed me. "What a moron," she sighed.

Dad told us, "After we give our condolences to Uncle Al, you don't have to go up to the casket if you don't want to."

Corinne asked, "Was her face run over?"

The woman ahead of us in line got all stiff-backed.

Mom took hold of Corinne's arm, and she dragged her out of the room.

"What?" We could hear Corinne's voice protesting. "What?"

Like an echo, "What?" Sophia demanded. The two of them are like . . . well, *twins.*

Dad put his finger to his lips, because Sophia

often needs to be reminded about the difference between an indoor voice and an outdoor voice. But he did answer Corinne's question. "There won't be anything wrong with Raquel's face."

"Moron," I muttered to Sophia. But I was glad to have Dad's reassurance.

After a couple minutes, Mom and Corinne returned. I was surprised that Mom just got back in line with us, but apparently cutting in a line at a funeral home is not as big a deal as cutting other times.

Corinne was sniffling, which she does any time she's reprimanded.

Mom rolled her eyes.

Sophia, who always takes Corinne's side, started whispering with her. Finally, together, the two of them asked, "Do we have to wait in line?"

"No." Mom and Dad answered in unison, too. "Just," Mom added, "remember where you are."

It was the girls' turn to roll their eyes.

We were getting close to the head of the line,

and I really didn't want to be there. "Can I go, too?" I asked.

Mom, busy trying to find a tissue in her purse, nodded and gestured me away.

I didn't head after the twins, who had spotted some of the girl cousins across the way and had gone to sit with them. It was just that I still had no idea what to say to Uncle Al. That, and I felt I was going to pass out because the room was so warm and so full of perfume, aftershave, and flowers. If I keeled over, I'd never hear the end of it. My embarrassment would go down in family folklore: "Remember the time . . . ?"

There were windows on the other side of the room, which were closed, but I thought maybe if I could just rest my hand against the glass, that would help me cool off.

I kept my head down as I approached to pass Raquel's coffin. Directly in front of it there was this kneeler thing, wide enough to hold two. A pair of girls about Raquel's age had been kneeling, praying,

I guess. But just as I was walking by, they stood, and we almost collided.

"Excuse me," they whispered in church voices. They walked around me.

I glanced back to where Uncle Al was talking to Great-aunt Gwen, my family not far behind. Nobody was in line for the kneeler.

I took a step closer.

The coffin itself was a dark wood, like Nona's china cabinet. The inside was pink satin.

Raquel doesn't like pink, I thought. I know this because Corinne and Sophia *love* pink. Their whole room is pink: pink walls, pink curtains, pink bedspreads—not matching, but pink, pink, pink. For their birthday in February, Raquel had bought them pink stuffed animals: a bear for Corinne, a dog for Sophia. "Pink fur goes against the natural laws of the universe," Raquel told them as, squealing with delight, they'd ripped open the wrappings and hugged the pink monstrosities. To me, privately, she'd added, "Being in their room is like being in a wad of bubble gum."

But now, lying in that pinkness, suddenly reminding me of Snow White in her casket, was Raquel.

I hadn't been planning on looking at her face, despite Dad's reassurance. But once I did, I couldn't look away.

I knelt down in front of the coffin.

Somebody had put makeup on her, which was not something I was used to seeing. Raquel didn't wear makeup—not even on special occasions, like at Christmas or for our cousin Jesse's wedding. But the funeral parlor people had forced a healthy pink glow onto her. Healthy but powdery, like the ancient aunts.

In life, her hair had had a tendency to be wild, and now it was unnaturally tamed. Her lips were thin and stretched out. And of course her eyes were closed.

People talk about pets being put to sleep, so I guess I'd assumed dead people would look like they were sleeping, but Raquel didn't look at all like she was asleep. In fact, she didn't quite look real. For some reason, I got the idea of candy in my mind: It was like she was made of spun sugar or something.

If she was a dessert or a mannequin, you'd say, "Wow, she looks so real!"

But you could tell the difference.

Not that I could think of any reason why they'd have substituted a spun sugar mannequin for Raquel, except just to spare me having to look at her.

That was stupid. I looked at her hands, folded quietly—and Raquel was never that still—and the hands were real. Not sugar, not even wax, or plaster or whatever they make mannequins out of.

And then I started thinking: It's still not really her. It was someone else, someone who looked a lot like Raquel, but it wasn't her. It was some other girl who'd been in an accident. And because she looked so much—but not exactly—like Raquel, people had gotten confused. They had told Uncle Al it was Raquel, and he'd been so upset, he hadn't taken a close enough look. It was sort of like with the story about the emperor's new clothes—where the emperor is naked, but everybody is convinced the problem is with themselves, that they're the only ones who can't see, so they don't want to admit anything. It was the same here. Everybody was probably thinking, *Hey, that doesn't even look like Raquel,* but nobody wanted to say so for fear of being stupid. It was sad that this other girl was dead, but this wasn't Raquel, who was really . . . who was really . . .

Where *was* Raquel?

Maybe, I thought, *maybe she was in an accident, too, except that she wasn't killed.* She was probably, at this very moment, lying in a hospital, suffering from amnesia, which was why she hadn't spoken up, and I would be the one who would be able to break the good news to the family, and we'd all go, like, "Whoa! That was a close one!" And I felt hands on my shoulders and Amorette was whispering into my ear, "Marco. Marco."

I realized I'd been leaning on the padded elbow rest, closer and closer to Raquel, my knees barely making contact with the kneeler. Because I'd been thinking of fairy tales, I figured I probably looked like I thought I was Prince Charming, like I thought I could kiss her awake. I *hope* I didn't look like that.

Uncle Al was there, too, having come to rest his hand on my head. He gazed down at Raquel, dead in her coffin.

"She wasn't a big fan of pink," I said.

"No," he agreed. Then he said, "They didn't have peppermint-striped."

That was how she'd painted her room: red and white stripes.

Uncle Al looked like he was going to cry because the lining was the wrong color.

"Well," I said, finally knowing what to say, "pink is like a melted peppermint."

Uncle Al patted my head again. "That's the way I'll think about it," he said.

"Yeah," I said.

Amorette said to me, "How about we go outside for some fresh air."

Which was uncommonly considerate of her. So I did.

Nona Falcone, Grandmother

I've watched Alzheimer's steal my husband's memories, one by one, from most recent to oldest—so that at the nursing home he'll say, "Hello," as though I haven't been holding his hand for the last half hour. He'll give the smile that won my heart in high school and say, "Thank you for visiting me. Do I know you?"

Oh, Raquel. Why did God bless him, and not me?

Hayley Evenski, Best Friend (Part 3)

I know a lot of the people here from my years of tagging along at so many Falcone family functions. I call them aunt and uncle as though they're related to me, just as Raquel adopted my parents' siblings. So I've been watching Uncle Ray get two of the younger cousins in trouble by wiggling his ears and making them giggle. Each time their mother turns around, Uncle Ray switches to a solemn face and the nephews get scolded.

Grandma Papadopulos can't stop crying, and periodically her daughters take her out—to the ladies' room, outside, I'm not sure. She comes back, seemingly composed, and then her eyes start leaking again.

Will I lose this family as truly as I've lost Raquel?

I feel numb.

Meanwhile, I'm watching a girl who is having a terrible time.

I saw her when she came in, and I took an immediate liking to her.

A lot of the other girls here are very chic in their little black dresses. You can tell they know they're looking good and that people are admiring them, and this makes it hard to take their subdued voices and somber faces seriously.

But this girl is dressed for the occasion without regard for the impression she makes on others. And given all the crocodile tears—or, let me be kind and call them self-indulgent tears—I've seen from the Quail Run kids tonight, this girl is a breath of fresh air.

We need fresh air in here, because the scent of the lilies is getting to be overwhelming.

Ever since we ended up going to separate schools in sixth grade, Raquel tried to keep me up on the goings-on, first at Maplewood Middle, then Quail Run. From her drawings, and from her descriptions, I'm pretty sure I've got Jonah Proia, Mara Ravenell, and Lindsay Lapjani pegged. I'm not certain—short of going over and demanding an introduction—how to tell the difference between two lovelies I assume are Zoe Kanisky and Stacy Galbo.

But, despite all these people whose identities I'm deducing, I don't have a name to put on this one girl.

She has started sneezing, and I suspect she is about to begin going through her purse again in search of a tissue. There's no telling what further catastrophe this might lead to, for—like Raquel—she obviously never cleans out her purse. So I grab one of the tissue boxes that are discreetly scattered about the room and sit down next to her.

She looks at me suspiciously, perhaps evaluating whether I might be the kind of jokester to sprinkle pepper into a box of tissues. It was Raquel who did that, not me. And only the one time. And it was at a family picnic, not a funeral.

But this girl is about to sneeze again, so she takes her chances. Perhaps she chooses to trust me and my tissues because that memory of Raquel has caught me unawares and now I'm sniffling, too.

"Thank you," she says.

After we're through blowing and wiping, I say, "You look like you've gotten into something your body doesn't like." Normally, I try not to be one of those people who is given to stating the obvious, but I figure this is a bit more tactful than saying, "Look at you! Do you need medical attention?" Instead, I tell her, "I have some cortisone cream in my purse."

"That," she tells me, "might be a big help."

I hand her a tube of the stuff for the rash that's starting, and give her a chewable allergy pill for the other symptoms.

"You must be a Girl Scout," she says.

Raquel and I never made it past Brownie level, and I'm not sure why she's saying this in any case.

Obviously I look as confused as I feel.

"'Be prepared,'" she clarifies.

"Ah," I tell her. "I'm pretty sure it's the Boy Scouts who say that, not the Girl Scouts."

"What do Girl Scouts say?" she asks.

I consider. "'Buy a cookie'?" I theorize.

The girl's face opens up into a smile, and she suddenly looks like a totally different person. I think I could like the person this smile reveals, so I suddenly find myself explaining how I myself am allergic to half the things in this room, then I go on to tell her about me and Raquel and the Brownie troop at Harborview Manor Nursing Home.

"I was never in the Brownies," this girl says. "But in fourth grade I had a civic-minded teacher who took us to the nursing home next door to the school—and we had similar results. Course, we were in the dementia wing, so it was even worse. One guy kept wanting to take his clothes off—luckily the aides kept almost on top of that situation. And there was this sweet-looking little old lady with her white hair in a bun and everything, the typical grandmother type, and she was swearing her head off. I guess Alzheimer's had brought out her inner sailor."

"Must be rough being stuck in a nursing home next to an elementary school," I say, making a mental note to put this in my living will: No incarceration in facilities that are within walking distance of anyone under the age of fourteen. I tell her, "My name is Hayley."

She says, "Vanessa."

"The writer?" I ask.

She gets that suspicious look again.

I say, "Raquel talked about a girl who wrote a funny column in the school paper."

Vanessa considers, then admits, "Well, I'm the only Vanessa, and I *do* write editorials for the paper when somebody is doing something stupid, which I guess means I write them on a pretty regular basis. Not that I was ever sure anybody actually read them. Raquel never said anything to me about them."

"Well, she was a bit shy. Not like me."

Vanessa asks, "You her sister?"

Which pretty much proves Raquel talked to me about Vanessa more than she talked to Vanessa about me.

"No. Raquel was an only child. I'm a friend." I realize I should be saying I *was* a friend. But even the thought of that makes my throat tighten up, and I realize my voice is coming from a teeny-tiny opening that's about to close up entirely. Vanessa and I wait for that to pass. Then I say, "We went to school together through fifth grade. But I'm just beyond the boundary for Maplewood, so I got sent to Governor Nelson Rockefeller Middle School. That was such a harrowing experience, my parents put me in Holy Name of Jesus for high school."

"But you kept in touch," Vanessa observes.

"Absolutely," I tell her. "Just about every weekend, either she would sleep over at my house, or I would sleep at hers. Then, of course, we were also part of the Sword of Mawrth online scene."

"Yeah?" she asks. Then admits, "I have no idea what you just said."

"It's a game. On the Internet. Each person has

his or her own persona. There are puzzles to solve, and adventures to share. You get to decide how to react to any given situation. People from all over the country play, and it's kind of neat. There's a real sense of community, even though most of the players never actually meet." Raquel would have said part of the joy of the game is that you can be somebody else, but I don't say this because I always told Raquel it was stupid: You can *look like* somebody else, you can give yourself a sexy name like Gylindrielle, you can provide yourself a background that's exciting or exotic or royal—but it's still you. Your persona can't be smarter than you or funnier than you or kinder than you, because you're the one who has to come up with what to say and do. What Sword of Mawrth did for Raquel was free her to be the person I always saw she was. Well, with a sword and a gold bustier and one incredible bod.

Vanessa, responding to the last thing I said out loud, about the community, says, "Sounds idyllic."

"Well, yeah, except for the brain-sucking demon hordes of Lord Lorenzo de Borgia."

"Hmmm," she says.

I know that if I do any more talking about Raquel, I'm likely to start crying. So I say, "Okay, I've told you a couple memories about Raquel—how about you tell me one?"

She considers. "She sat in front of me in homeroom."

I wait, then realize there's no more to come.

She says, "I hardly knew her."

"But you came here . . . ," I say. Her eyes are no longer watering, and the rash is beginning to calm down, but I can still finish, ". . . at substantial personal inconvenience."

Vanessa looks off into the distance, and I think she's seen someone she knows and is about to ditch me, but then she makes eye contact again and says, "I didn't think anyone would come. I didn't think she had any friends—she certainly didn't seem to have any at Quail Run—and I thought her parents would be sitting here, just them and her, listening to the clock tick, hearing the front door open and someone coming in, but it's always for the person laid out in the room down the hall." She looks away again and doesn't tell me if this happened to someone she knew, or if she's afraid it will happen to her. She inclines her head toward the girl—it's got to be Mara Ravenell—who's having people sign her petition. "Little did I expect this circus."

"Raquel would have loved it," I tell her.

This girl, Vanessa, reminds me so much of Raquel. When I say, "Raquel would have loved it," I mean only because it's *for* Raquel. Otherwise, she'd be as pissed off at everyone as Vanessa seems to be on Raquel's behalf.

But I've gotten distracted. I figure most of the people I don't know are from Quail Run. Besides the students, I've also picked out a few of the teachers, including Mrs. Bellanca, Raquel's English teacher, who—true to her word at the beginning of the year—always gave Raquel an extra three points on any paper where Raquel drew a picture.

But a member of the Quail Run staff whom I personally know has just come into the room.

I whip my glasses off so I won't have to see her,

although in theory that would make me more easily recognizable to her. Not that I believe Mrs. Scarborough would ever remember me just because she made my life wretched in first grade. I duck my head behind the flower arrangement Vanessa tangled with earlier.

"What?" Vanessa asks.

"Mrs. Scarborough."

"Yeah?" Vanessa is giving me that oh-dear-and-here-I-was-thinking-you-were-normal look. "She's the library media assistant."

"Yes, but before that she was a nasty, nasty first-grade teacher," I correct her.

"That," Vanessa says, "would explain a lot."

Sword of Mawrth Boards

SATURDAY/07:15PMCDT

WARRIORGUY: Hey, has anyone heard from Gylindrielle? She hasn't been here, and she hasn't added to her blog in days. Comet Girl, have you heard anything? Anyone?

Patricia Saye-Evans, Emergency Medical Technician

I recently watched my mother die.

It took a long time. A long, hard time.

I'd asked her to make a living will, or to fill out a do-not-resuscitate order. She said, "Oh, honey, I can't. I'll leave it up to you. You make the right decision for me when the time comes."

But when the time came, I wasn't there. My sister was.

We had talked about it, Rosemary and I. Mom was old-school religion, I'd explained to Rosemary, when she came from Boston to stay with Mom when we saw the end was near. Mom wasn't sure it was right to sign a document saying she did not want to be kept alive by artificial means because she was afraid that might be akin to suicide. She wanted us to choose for her. "This is what she wants," I told Rosemary. "Every time there's something in the news about a case where a family can't decide, Mom always says, 'They should let her go. It's cruel not to let her go.'" I said to Rosemary, "That's what she wants. She just can't come out and say it."

Rosemary cried, but said she understood. Said she agreed.

But when Mom flatlined, Rosemary panicked. She screamed for the doctors and demanded they do something.

"Are you sure?" the floor nurse asked, because we had talked to her, too.

And Rosemary, weeping, said, "Yes."

So they brought in the crash cart and the paddles, and after three shocks to Mom's poor, wisplike body, they got her heart going again.

They had to intubate her after that, and give her a morphine drip. Mom couldn't talk anymore, but her eyes were terrified.

Rosemary, fragile soul, couldn't take more than a week of it and returned to Boston, back home to her husband and children, leaving me to sit by Mom's side.

So when, at that accident scene on Poscover, while I was working over that poor broken girl—when the police officer shook the contents of her purse out onto the sidewalk in his search for ID, and that DNR order came fluttering out of the notebook she carried, I knew what to do. It wasn't signed. A girl her age—it wouldn't have been legal even if it *was* signed. She must have known that. She must have seen someone close to her go through something like my mother did, and she didn't want the same thing to happen to her.

With her injuries, the most I could have given her was another day, and the best I could have hoped for that day would be that she would spend it unconscious. For an EMT, there's things you can do and Things You Can Do.

I let her slip away.

Albert Falcone, Father (Part 2)

Father Kevin has just finished telling me that—though the time God has given us on earth is short because we were created to spend eternity with Him in heaven—it is always sad to lose one *so* young.

I appreciate that Father Kevin is trying to console me.

But "*sad*"?

I thought when Cleo died my heart had died along with her. But now I see I was wrong.

With my wife dying and then my daughter, it's like my own life has been negated. I suddenly realize I have no purpose. Forty-two years of my taking up space on this earth—for what? To keep my company's books straight? To keep the patch of lawn at 432 Williams Street well tended between the Steinmillers, who lived there before, and whoever will move in after I've gone?

When Cleo died in December, I thought: *I must be strong for Raquel.*

There's nobody to be strong for now. There's nobody to *be* for now.

Raquel took her mom's death so hard.

We had been up front with her all along, telling her the numbers for this particular cancer were not good, but Raquel wouldn't believe it.

"You've got to be strong," Raquel would tell her mother. "You've got to fight it."

Like the cancer was a villain from one of those fantasy books she loved. Like there was a way to vanquish it if we just stayed pure of heart and searched hard enough and endured a certain number of hardships on the way. Well, Cleo *was* pure of heart, and the hardships to be endured were the chemo and the radiation—but in the end nothing was enough.

Raquel was a smart girl. She knew the difference between fiction and real life. But she couldn't believe there was nothing we could do—she thought there had to be some alternative medicine or experimental treatment. She became angry with her mother for giving up, when in truth Cleo simply came to accept what was happening.

I remember Cleo asking me to get a do-not-resuscitate order from the nurse. "I've asked her several times," Cleo said. "I know my memory's not good with all these drugs, but I'm sure I have, and she keeps saying she's left one with me, but she never does."

I went and got one from the nurse, and held it while Cleo, barely able to grasp the pen, signed.

Raquel was furious.

We tried to explain that all it meant was that the doctors would not take heroic measures to prolong Cleo's life.

"Why don't we just take her out to the ditch behind our house and shoot her?" Raquel demanded.

Despite her own pain, Cleo recognized that

Raquel was speaking from a pain of her own. By then Cleo, who had always been so pink and round and beautiful, was pale and haggard, with her skin-and-bones frame bruised black and purple and yellow from all the different needles. Her voice was thready and hoarse. "Honey," Cleo said, "I'm going to hold on for as long as I can. This just says that they won't jam a feeding tube up my nose when I'm unconscious, or keep my lungs going with a ventilator, or restart my heart if it stops."

"Those kinds of things happen all the time," Raquel said. "And then people recover."

"But this is if I'm not going to recover." Cleo tried to take Raquel's hand, but the IV line gave her limited reach, and Raquel stood and moved to the window, keeping her back to us.

"You never know," Raquel said. "Not for sure. People are always talking about miracle cures. Are you saying you don't believe in God?"

If you don't believe in God at any other time, you have to believe at a time like then, or you would go crazy.

Cleo barely had the strength to keep her eyes open, much less reason with Raquel. So I said, "We all believe."

I thought Cleo had fallen asleep, but then she whispered, "It's just if God wants to cure me, he'd better do it before my heart stops, or before I need a feeding tube."

Raquel said, "That's barbaric."

But by then Cleo truly had fallen asleep.

When I went through Raquel's room yesterday, looking for mementos to bring here to the funeral parlor—photographs, pictures she'd drawn, her certificate from Odyssey of the Mind from fifth grade—when I was going through her things, I came across three do-not-resuscitate orders. There was also the one that was in her notebook that night. As well as the one they found in her locker. Orders that she had taken from the hospital bedside table so that her mother couldn't sign them—couldn't give up.

Raquel would *never* give up.

Vanessa Weiss, Classmate (Part 3)

Mrs. Scarborough is carrying a huge purse. "Oh," I say to Hayley, "I hope she hasn't brought Miss Hap with her."

"Who?"

I find it hard to believe Mrs. Scarborough didn't have Miss Hap in first grade but has her now for high school. "Miss Hap," I repeat in case Hayley simply didn't hear me. "Her puppet?"

Hayley shakes her head.

"She has this puppet that talks to the students about things."

"Things?"

"Like about being sensitive toward people who

have disabilities or those of different ethnic backgrounds. Like about not bullying or giving in to peer pressure."

Hayley says, "You are kidding, right?"

I hold my hand up to shoulder level and flap my fingers to simulate a mouth moving. Keeping my voice soft, so as not to be disrespectful of Raquel's relatives, I still pitch the tone high and say, "Always treat others the way you'd like to be treated."

Hayley tries, with only moderate success, to cover a snorting laugh.

"Oooh," I continue, "think how you're making Miss Hap feel by acting that way."

Hayley sinks lower into the cushions of her chair and covers her face with her hands.

"And remember," I have my hand lecture, "never, never let boys touch you in a way that makes you feel uncomfortable."

Hayley's shoulders are shaking, and she's making shushing motions with her hands, though she's making more noise than I am.

An older couple who had drifted close by gives us looks like we're publicly picking our noses.

"What?" my hand asks.

Hayley grabs my wrist and shoves my hand under a couple pillows. "Die," she orders in a whisper. "Die, die, die."

I let my hand go limp.

She peels back one of the pillows, and I let my hand flutter. She covers it again.

"Miss Hap has had a mishap," I announce.

"Good," Hayley says. She wipes her eyes and puts her glasses back on and looks for Mrs. Scarborough. "She doesn't really?" she asks me.

" 'Fraid so."

"I can't believe Raquel never told me."

"I think Raquel avoided the library," I say, "now that I think about it. Mrs. Shesman, the head librarian, is in charge of the newspaper, so I was always going in there because of the articles I was writing. I guess I had more contact with Mrs. Scarborough than most of the students would have. Mrs. Scarborough is only part-time, you know?

Mornings, she's at Rockefeller Middle, and we'll give her the benefit of the doubt that Miss Hap is mostly for them."

"She's gone over to Rockefeller?" Hayley asks in horror. "I got out of there just in time."

"So what was she like as a first-grade teacher?"

Hayley tells how she needed glasses, and Mrs. Scarborough was oblivious, and Raquel helped her out. "I just don't understand it," she ends. "I would have thought you and Raquel would have been great friends."

"I don't understand it, either," I say, because I've been thinking the same thing. I don't know why we didn't click except that, as Hayley said, she was shy. And I'm not exactly outgoing, either.

"Oh no, oh no, oh no," Hayley suddenly gasps. "She's opening her bag."

But Mrs. Scarborough isn't bringing out the dreaded Miss Hap. She's bringing out what looks like a cookie tin.

"Snacks?" Hayley asks incredulously.

Mrs. Scarborough demands everyone's attention. She summons us to come closer and, in fascinated horror, Hayley and I comply.

Holding on to my self-destructing skirt so that it doesn't migrate to the South Pole, I whisper to Hayley, "You don't happen to have a safety pin, do you?"

Not only does she have one in that well-stocked purse of hers, but she knows exactly where it is and has it in my hand in under five seconds.

I have just finished securing myself when Mrs. Scarborough announces, "I have a little project here, to help commemorate and memorialize Raquel's life."

Hayley makes an exaggerated disappointed expression and mouths the words, *Not snacks.*

As she apparently was in first grade, Mrs. Scarborough is yet again oblivious to Hayley, and she says, "I have had my middle school students construct these paper butterflies for us tonight." She opens the tin and plucks out a parchment butterfly that is about the size of my hand. "What I'd like each of you to do is to take a butterfly . . ."—she starts handing them out, and I see that they are in a variety of colors, besides the off-white of regular parchment, also pink and pale blue and green and fuschia and turquoise—"and take a pen . . ."—she has brought a multitude of those, too—"and I want you to write a message to Raquel."

Hayley quirks an eyebrow, and several others in the crowd are just as confused and start asking questions.

Mrs. Scarborough explains, "You can tell her something you maybe didn't have a chance to say to her, or you can maybe tell her something you liked about her, or something you wish you could say to her, something to celebrate her life."

"Are you going to read these out loud?" Ned Freeman asks.

"No," Mrs. Scarborough answers in a tone Ned probably hasn't heard since *he* was in first grade, "these are messages for Raquel. We'll write to her, then we'll collect the butterflies in this fireproof tin, then we'll step outside, where I've made arrangements with the staff here, and we'll burn the papers, so that the smoke—and our good wishes for Raquel—goes up into the night sky."

Somehow or other I have ended up standing next to Mrs. Bellanca, who mutters, "Talk about your mixed metaphors," and I suddenly find myself liking her a whole lot better than I ever have before.

Despite Mrs. Bellanca's negativism, most of the people seem to think the butterflies are a fine idea.

Hayley snags two of them, and I think that it's because—as Raquel's best friend—she has a lot to say. But after writing a bit, she hands one to me, and I see that what she's written on that one is her phone number and a Web URL, which I take to be the Sword of Mawrth gaming site.

"Just in case you're interested," she says.

And—just in case I *am*—I put the butterfly in my purse.

Mrs. Scarborough's Butterfly Project

Hey Raquel

Sorry I never got to know you.

You were a wonderful artist.

You had very pretty eyes.

I always liked those sandals you wore—you know, the ones with the sparkles?

Um, this is so stupid.

Thanks for being our friend.
Thank you for the white feather.
If you can, call me. On my cell phone. That would be *so* neat.
We'll get that speed limit down.
Hope you like the flowers.
Peaceful journey, Gylindrielle.
I'm so sorry.
Stay safe, baby girl.